To Paolo,
fellow troublemaker!
—J. A.

SIMON & SCHUSTER BOOKS FOR YOUNG READERS
An imprint of Simon & Schuster Children's Publishing Division
1230 Avenue of the Americas, New York, New York 10020
Text copyright © 2014 by Joanna Walsh
Illustrations copyright © 2014 by Giuditta Gaviraghi
Originally published in Great Britain in 2014 by Simon & Schuster UK Ltd.
Published by arrangement with Simon & Schuster UK Ltd.
First US edition 2014
SIMON & SCHUSTER BOOKS FOR YOUNG READERS is a trademark of Simon & Schuster, Inc.
For information about special discounts for bulk purchases, please contact Simon & Schuster Special Sales
at 1-866-506-1949 or business@simonandschuster.com.
The Simon & Schuster Speakers Bureau can bring authors to your live event. For more information or to book an event,
contact the Simon & Schuster Speakers Bureau at 1-866-248-3049 or visit our website at www.simonspeakers.com.
The text for this book is set in Artcraft URW T.
Manufactured in China
0914 SCP
2 4 6 8 10 9 7 5 3 1
Library of Congress Cataloging-in-Publication Data
Walsh, Joanna.
I love Mom / Joanna Walsh ; illustrated by Judi Abbot.
pages cm
Summary: Animal characters celebrate mothers, especially ones who play fun games, have bright smiles, and kiss hurt knees.
ISBN 978-1-4814-2808-8 (hardback)
ISBN 978-1-4814-2838-5 (eBook)
[1. Stories in rhyme. 2. Mothers—Fiction. 3. Animals—Fiction.] I. Abbot, Judi, illustrator. II. Title.
PZ8.3.W1932Iam 2014
[E]—dc23
2014007180

I Love Mom

Joanna Walsh

Illustrated by Judi Abbot

A Paula Wiseman Book
Simon & Schuster Books for Young Readers
New York London Toronto Sydney New Delhi

Some smiles are sun smiles,
run-for-miles smiles,
but no one's smile is wider, brighter,
than my **mom's** smile.

Some games are fun games, but not like **Mom's** games.

She can make a paper plate
into a plane,

a couple of cups into a telephone,

a chair
into a throne,

an umbrella
into a slide trombone!

But who'd have guessed
a mess could be
so quick to pick up,

a box so quick to pack up?

Count to ten, sit on the lid,
there, done!

What's next?

Nobody bakes so cake-y,

no sticky mix so yummy
(crumbs!) as mommy's.

But while it's in the oven
there's a dozen other bothers.

Whether it's one
  or another
    or all together,

nobody juggles them like **Mom** till—

ding!—the baking's done!

When we go out
she slips her hand in mine.

No other mother looks so fine.

No one strolling up the street
so neat, so pretty.

And at the park nobody
swings my swing so high.

No one brings the sky
closer to the seesaw.

No one else sees
(down on our knees)
the tiny beasts creep
'cept her and me.

But if we fight

nobody else can take a wrong
and make a right.

No tears for a hurt knee or feelings
could be kissed better.

And when we set off back,
no long, long way home

so snail-slow,
could go so quick.

No hop
no skip
so slick

over our front doorstep—

to get us home in time to eat.

And then . . .

. . . no bath splash could be wetter.
No water jet, set to get her back,

is such a laugh.

No rub's more cuddly than **Mom's** towel hug.

No jammies are so warm or so snuggly.

No tucking-in so dozy
no toes so cozy,
no good-night kiss so right—

good night, **Mom**.
Good night.